Where's My Mummy?

For the Fruits —
Janie Bynum, Kelly DiPucchio, Hope Vestergaard,
Lisa Wheeler, Paula Yoo, and April Young Fritz
C. C.

For Mom
J. M.

ISBN-13: 978-0-545-20131-5
ISBN-10: 0-545-20131-4

Text copyright © 2008 by Carolyn Crimi.
Illustrations copyright © 2008 by John Manders. All rights reserved.
Published by Scholastic Inc., 557 Broadway, New York, NY 10012, by
arrangement with Candlewick Press. SCHOLASTIC and associated logos are
trademarks and/or registered trademarks of Scholastic Inc.

12 11 10 9 8 7 6 5 4 3 2 1   9 10 11 12 13 14/0

Printed in the U.S.A.   40

This edition first printing, September 2009

This book was typeset in LittleGrog.
The illustrations were done in gouache.

Where's My Mummy?

Carolyn Crimi

illustrated by John Manders

SCHOLASTIC INC.
New York Toronto London Auckland
Sydney Mexico City New Delhi Hong Kong

On a deep, dark night in a deep, dark place, Little Baby Mummy did not want to go to bed.

"Just one more game of Hide and Shriek?" he pleaded to Big Mama Mummy. "Count your bandages while I hide!"

Little Baby Mummy ran—

and hid—

and waited, until . . .

"Mama Mummy, where are you?"
He looked over graves and he looked
over tombs, but Big Mama Mummy was
nowhere to be found.

So he tromped, tromped, tromped
to the deep, dark woods, the spookery
woods, to look for Big Mama Mummy.
He stopped and he listened.

Clank clink clank
Woo boo woo
Clank clink CLOO

"Mama Mummy, is that you?"
But out of the woods clanked—

BONES!

"You're not my mummy!"

Bones was brushing his clicky-clack teeth. "Little Baby Mummy, go to bed!" he said. "There are creatures that bite in the deep, dark night." Then he gargled with goo.

"I'm not scared!"

Little Baby Mummy tromped, tromped, tromped to the deep, dark swamp, the slithery swamp, to look for Big Mama Mummy.

He stopped and he listened.

Glug glug glip
Glug glug glop
Glug glug GLOO

"Mama Mummy, is that you?"
But out of the swamp slid—

"You're not my mummy!"
Glob shook his wiggly, wobbly head.
"Little Baby Mummy, go to bed!" he
said. "There are creatures that creep
in the deep, dark night." And he washed
the gunk off his ooey, gooey face.

"I'm not scared!"

Little Baby Mummy tromped, tromped, tromped to the deep, dark cave, the shivery cave, to look for Big Mama Mummy.

He stopped and he listened.

Flap flip flap
Whap whap WHOO
Flap flip FLOO

"Mama Mummy, is that you?"
But out of the cave whooshed—

"You're not my mummy!"

Drac flapped his flippy, floppy wings. "Little Baby Mummy, go to bed!" he said. "There are creatures that swoop in the deep, dark night." Then he scrubbed his long, pointy ears.

"I'm not scared!"
Little Baby Mummy plunked down
under a creaky, squeaky tree.
"Mama Mummy, where are you?"
He stopped and he listened.

Rustle rustle rustle
Scritch scratch scritch
Rustle rustle rustle

"Mama Mummy, are you there?"
But out of the tree popped—

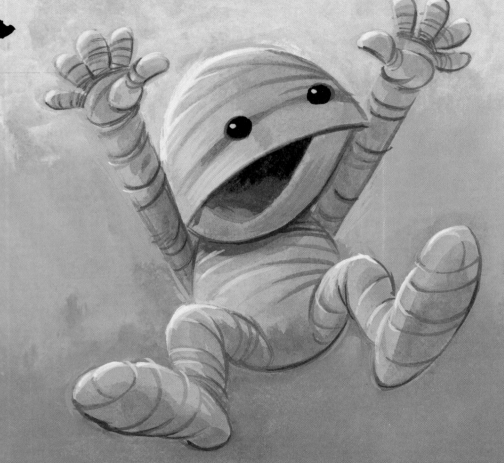

"I'M HERE!" cried Big Mama Mummy.

Little Baby Mummy
and Big Mama Mummy
tromped back home,

where they brushed
and combed

and gargled and
scrubbed.

Then Big Mama Mummy wrapped
Little Baby Mummy up tight.
And he slept and he snored for the
rest of the night. . . .

Wee wee wee
Snoo snoo snoo
Wee wee SNOO!